Campbell

Liam

Liya

Callum

Benjamin

Josh

Charlie

Thank you to Orchard Fields
Community School, Banbury
for helping with the endpapers.

For my dear sister Moya—V.T.

For Willow Floyd Söderström Paul,
with love—K.P.

OXFORD
UNIVERSITY PRESS

Great Clarendon Street, Oxford OX2 6DP

Oxford University Press is a department of the
University of Oxford. It furthers the University's
objective of excellence in research, scholarship,
and education by publishing worldwide.
Oxford is a registered trade mark of
Oxford University Press in the UK and
n certain other countries

Text copyright © Valerie Thomas 2018
Illustrations copyright © Korky Paul 2018
The moral rights of the author and artist
have been asserted

Database right Oxford University Press (maker)

First published in 2018

British Library Cataloguing in Publication Data available

ISBN: 978-0-19-276693-9 (hardback)

10 9 8 7 6 5 4 3 2 1

Printed in China

Paper used in the production of this book is a natural, recyclable
product made from wood grown in sustainable forests. The
manufacturing process conforms to the environmental
regulations of the country of origin

www.winnieandwilbur.com

VALERIE THOMAS AND KORKY PAUL

Winnie and Wilbur
THE MONSTER MYSTERY

OXFORD

UNIVERSITY PRESS

Winnie the Witch and her big black cat Wilbur lived in a black house in the forest. They had lived there for years and years and years.

When Winnie and Wilbur first moved in, it was quite a small forest. But the trees grew and grew until they almost covered the house.

'We should trim some of these trees, Wilbur,' Winnie would say. 'They make the house and garden so dark.'

But she never did.

There were birds and squirrels and foxes and rabbits living in the forest. In fact anything could have been living in the forest, it was so thick and dark . . .

One morning Winnie noticed big footprints in the garden.

'I wonder who made those footprints, Wilbur,' Winnie said. 'Perhaps we should go and have a look.' It could be a big hairy monster, thought Wilbur. He didn't want to go into the forest and look.

But Winnie had started to walk into the forest,
so Wilbur ran after her.
Winnie was not enjoying the walk.
Brambles caught in her clothes and hair, a sharp branch poked her nose,

and she tripped over a tree root and fell into a prickle bush.

'Blithering broomsticks!' shouted Winnie.
'We'll never see anything hiding in here.'

Then Winnie had a good idea.
'I know what we'll do, Wilbur,' she said.
'We'll fly over the forest and look down.'

Wilbur leaned over to have a look and . . . slipped off Winnie's shoulder.

He bounced from branch to branch,

Winnie jumped onto her broomstick, Wilbur jumped onto her shoulder and they zoomed up into the air.

But the forest was so thick and dark they couldn't see through the trees. 'Can you see anything, Wilbur?' asked Winnie.

and then landed
on something . . .

. . . soft and hairy.
A BIG hairy monster.

'Meow! Meow!' cried Wilbur.
He was frightened.

There were big hairy monsters all around him.
They patted Wilbur and picked the
leaves and prickles out of his fur.

Then they gently put him down on the ground . . .

. . . in between their tiny feet.

They were big friendly hairy
monsters with tiny feet!
So they weren't leaving those
big footprints in the garden.

Winnie flew round and round the forest.
She was worried about Wilbur.

Where was he?

She had to find him. But how?

Then she had a very good idea.

She landed her broomstick on the
far edge of the forest,
waved her magic wand,
shouted,

'Abracadabra!'

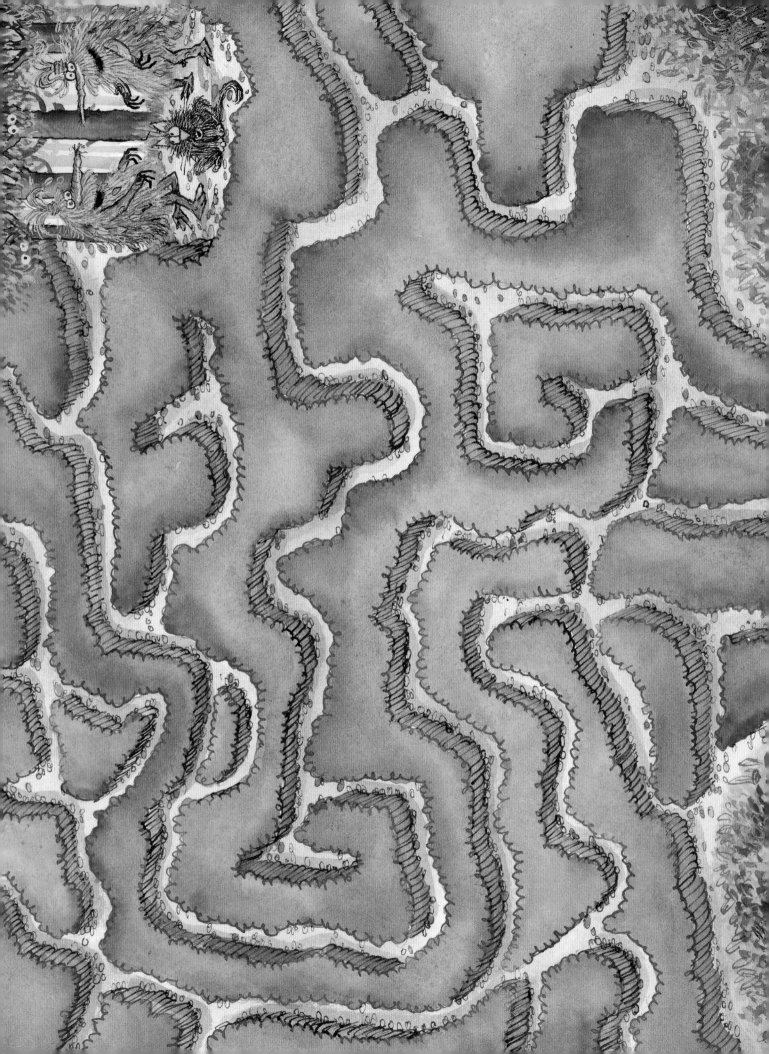

. . . and there was a path
winding through the forest.
And another path.
And another path.

'Wilbur!' called Winnie.
'Where are you? Wilbur! Wilbur!'

Wilbur heard her.
So did the monsters. They crept
back into the trees.

Wilbur ran to meet Winnie.
She was delighted to see him.

'I've been so worried, Wilbur,'
said Winnie. 'Let's go home.'

'Purr, purr, purr,'
said Wilbur.

Winnie waved
her magic wand,
shouted,

'Abracadabra!'

. . . and the paths disappeared.

'That's better,' Winnie said.
'But it's a pity the forest is
making our house so dark.
I'd like the sun to shine in.'

Then Winnie had an excellent idea.
She waved her magic wand, shouted,

'Abracadabra!'

. . . and Winnie's house and garden moved
out of the forest and into the sunshine.

The next morning Winnie put on her
big gardening boots and went out to
get a pumpkin for her pumpkin soup.

At lunchtime, while Winnie and Wilbur were
having their pumpkin soup, Winnie saw big
footprints going right across the grass.

'There they are again, Wilbur,' Winnie said. 'I don't suppose we'll ever find out who's been making those footprints.'

'Meeow!' said Wilbur. He knew *exactly* who was making those footprints!

Reece

Elisha

Layla

Zeshan

Pawel

Nathan

Rhys